Clara's Christmas Miracle

by Shirley Graves

For Christopher-Conrad Robinson

Illustrations by Felle Jones

Cover by Dan Swanson of www.van-garde.com

ISBN13: 978-0-9641959-2-9

Clara, the cookie jar, is a well-loved and happy cookie jar.

Clara has a wonderful family—Mom, Dad, Sheila, and Jeremy. She has been a part of their family for as long as Sheila and Jeremy can remember.

Family and friends often come to visit. Clara loves having cookies for them. They look forward to enjoying these cookies.

The Christmas season is Clara's favorite time of year. She loves the good cheer and festive decorations.

Sheila and Jeremy like helping Mom bake holiday cookies and decorating them.

Christmas carolers are always eager to stop by for cider and the fancy Christmas cookies that Clara has to offer.

Now, this Christmas is going to be an especially exciting one. Their new home will be finished in time for a Christmas move.

Everything is wrapped and packed—including Clara. Mom assures Sheila and Jeremy that Clara will arrive safely.

Sheila and Jeremy leave with Mom and Dad to meet the moving truck at their new home.

The moving truck travels along at a safe speed. Suddenly, a squirrel darts in the path of the moving truck. It swerves to avoid hitting the squirrel.

This causes some of the boxes to tumble out and roll down a hill, including Clara's box.

All of the boxes were collected and placed back in the truck—all of the boxes except Clara's box.

Clara's box rolled further away. It was hidden behind a large tree and was difficult to see.

Sheila and Jeremy are eagerly awaiting the arrival of the moving truck.

All of the boxes are unloaded,
but Clara is not there.

The driver explains to them what happened. He tells them that they repacked all of the boxes. They thought that Clara was among those boxes.

Dad agrees to take Sheila and Jeremy
to search for Clara.

They search for Clara in that area, but cannot find her. "I'm over here," cries Clara. But they cannot hear her.

Sheila and Jeremy return home without Clara. They are very disappointed. Grandma offers to buy them a new cookie jar. But a new cookie jar is not the same as Clara.

One morning, Mr. Jenkins was walking his dog. The dog began to bark when it approached a tree. Mr. Jenkins went to have a look. There was a box with no label on it.

Mr. Jenkins was surprised to find a cookie jar inside. He tried to find out whom the cookie jar belonged to, but without success. He decided to donate the cookie jar to the annual Christmas fundraiser bazaar.

Clara is placed on a table with other items for sale. Clara hears the Christmas music and she thinks of her family. She thinks of her past happy Christmas days. People buy other items, but no one buys Clara.

Clara longs to be with her family. She knows that it would take a miracle for this to happen, but Clara believes in miracles. Clara had heard that Christmas was a time of miracles. Maybe—just maybe—she would have her own Christmas miracle.

At home, something seems missing this Christmas season. It is not the same without Clara. There is no fun in baking and decorating the cookies.

Mom tries to cheer up Sheila and Jeremy when they cannot find Clara. She decides to take them to the Christmas bazaar, which is always fun.

Everything reminds them of Clara. Since they aren't having a good time, they tell Mom that they want to leave. As they are about to leave, they walk by one last table on their way to the door.

There, tucked in a corner, is Clara. They cannot believe what they are seeing. "Clara," they cry in unison, "is that really you?" Clara is excited to see them, too.

Clara goes home with them, where she belongs. Christmas seems special again. They decorate their home and bake their cookies.

Clara is especially happy and thankful. She knows that a Christmas miracle has truly taken place.

CPSIA information can be obtained
at www.ICGtesting.com
Printed in the USA
LVIC04n1729151014
408913LV00005B/13

* 9 780964 195929 *